Pickled!

Written by
LuShanna Houston

Pickled

Published By LuShanna Houston

****

ISBN: 979-8-218-26499-4

This book is dedicated to all my present and future grannybabies!

It was a nice and sunny day in the spring when a seed was placed in the ground.

After about 4 weeks (a month)
up from the ground burst a vine.
It was green, curvy, and it felt
kind of hairy.

On this vine were two cucumbers.
One of the cucumbers was
long, slim, hard, and light green.
The other cucumber was
short, plump, hard, and dark green.

Crispy and Crunchy played in the garden
with their vegetable friends...
Curlie Carrot, Tickled Tomato, and Head of Lettuce,
just to name a few.

All the friends laughed and could hardly wait, all except Crunchy.

Crunchy wanted the same opportunities as Crispy and their vegetable friends, but he didn't want to take the same path to success as they had in mind.

Crunchy even wanted to be loved by everybody,
but Crunchy did not want to attend the "College of Salad."

"Oh, what can I do!" thought Crunchy.
Crunchy felt a little sad.
It was kind of hot that day,
so Crunchy decided to go for a dip (swim) in the kiddie pool.

Crunchy laid there thinking and drifted off to sleep.

As Crunchy slept, the sun was beaming (shinning) down on the pool and the water began to get hot.

Crunchy was in such a deep sleep dreaming about his future,
he didn't realize how hot the water had become.

Finally, after a few hours, Crunchy woke up feeling a little different.

Crunchy noticed his reflection (image) in the water.
He was still short, plump and dark green, but he was no longer hard but a little soft!

"Oh, my goodness, what happened to me, I've changed, I'm no longer a cucumber!"
said Crunchy, excitingly.

I can be sweet or sour!

I can be spicy (hot) or dill!

Can you guess what I've become,
while I was out in the pool of hot water for all of those hours?

"I'm a Pickle !"

Crunchy was so excited he began to dance and sing.
I can't imagine all the joy I will bring.
I can go on a lot of things.
I can go in a lot of things.

I can go on all types of sandwiches, in relishes and in salads.

WOW!
You can put me on hotdogs and peanut butter and jelly sandwiches.

You can put me in cakes, pies and cookies.

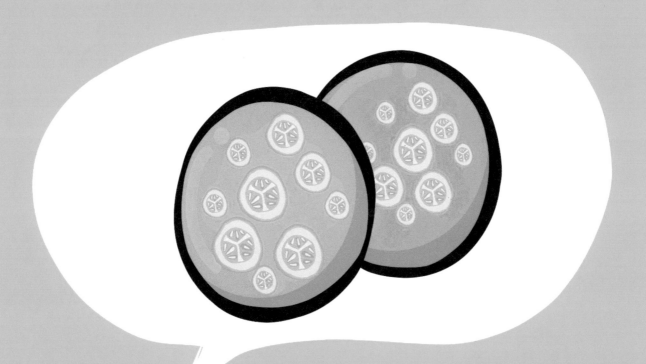

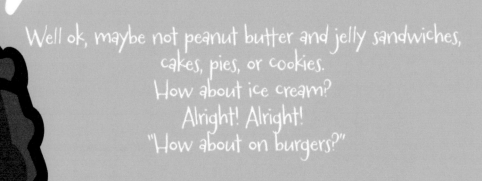

Well ok, maybe not peanut butter and jelly sandwiches,
cakes, pies, or cookies.
How about ice cream?
Alright! Alright!
"How about on burgers?"

"I've been changed. Now don't think it's strange.
I'm no longer a cucumber, but a pickle.
I'm going to be the best that I can be.
I will be successful and everybody will love me."

Pickled Props

The moral of the story is that you can come from the same place,
have some of the same dreams of becoming successful,
but you might fulfill them at a different time and or way.
As long as, you can use your imagination (in which we all can),
work hard and you can see yourself doing whatever you imagine,
then your dreams can come true.
What can children learn from this book?
What is success?
What does it mean to be successful?
Life cycle of a pickle
The different kinds of vegetables and how they come about
What are some of the ways vegetables can be prepared
Different words with similar meanings
Healthy and unhealthy foods
Opposites, Textures, Flavors
Inspirational, Encouraging, Funny, Entertaining
Days of the week
Months

About the Author

LuShanna Houston

LuShanna Houston is a lover of GOD and all HIS people. She enjoys giving and receiving hugs, motivating, and creating. She follows in the footsteps of her late mother Earlean Rainey, who dreamed of becoming an educator of children. LuShanna never planned to become an educator of children, but GOD had HIS Plan. LuShanna has been an educator for twenty rewarding and exciting years.

Acknowledgements

Thank GOD for EVERYTHING!
Thanks to my family and friends for the
love, encouragement, and support.
Thanks to T.Y. Somerville for her skills,
time, attention, and patience.
Thanks to an absolutely amazing artist,
Devante Woodson.